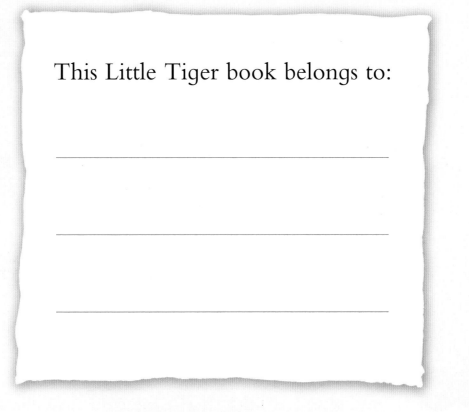

This Little Tiger book belongs to:

_____

_____

_____

For Flora, Ron and Elaine
~J S

For Glen P
~T W

LITTLE TIGER PRESS LTD,
an imprint of the Little Tiger Group
1 Coda Studios, 189 Munster Road, London SW6 6AW
www.littletiger.co.uk

First published in Great Britain 1996
This edition published 2017

Printed in China • LTP/1400/2927/0819

ISBN 978-1-84869-755-3

4 6 8 10 9 7 5 3

I don't want to go to bed!

Julie Sykes
Tim Warnes

 LiTTLE TiGER
LONDON

Little Tiger was very naughty.
He did not like going to bed.
Every night when Mummy Tiger
said, "Bedtime!"
Little Tiger would say,
"But I don't *want* to go to bed!"

Little Tiger wouldn't let Mummy Tiger clean his face
and paws, and he wouldn't listen to his bedtime story.
    One night Mummy Tiger lost her temper.
When Little Tiger said, "I don't want to go to bed!"
Mummy Tiger roared,
"ALL RIGHT, YOU CAN STAY UP ALL NIGHT THEN!"

Little Tiger couldn't believe his good luck.
He scampered off into the jungle before
Mummy Tiger could change her mind.

Little Tiger went to visit his
best friend, Little Lion.
When he arrived,
Little Lion was having
his ears washed.

"It's bedtime," growled Daddy Lion.
"Why are you still up?"

"I don't want to go to bed!" said Little
Tiger, and he skipped off into
the jungle before Daddy Lion
could wash his ears, too!

Little Tiger decided to visit his second best friend, Little Hippo.

He found him splashing in the river, having a bedtime bath.

"It's bedtime," bellowed Daddy Hippo.
"Why are you still up?"
  "I don't want to go to bed!" said Little Tiger,
and he scurried off into the jungle before
Daddy Hippo could give him a bath, too!

Little Elephant was Little Tiger's third best friend.
He went to visit him next.

Little Elephant was not out playing.
He was in bed, listening to his bedtime story.

"It's bedtime," trumpeted Mummy Elephant.
"Why are you still up?"

"I don't want to go to bed!" said Little Tiger,
and he bounced off into the jungle before
Mummy Elephant could put him to bed, too!

Little Tiger thought he
would go and find
Little Monkey,
his fourth best friend.
But he found Mummy
Monkey first. She put
a finger to her lips and
whispered, "Little
Monkey is fast asleep.
Why are you still up?"

"I don't want to go to bed!"
Little Tiger whispered back.
Quickly he tiptoed into the
jungle before Mummy Monkey
made him fall asleep, too!

Little Tiger didn't know where to go next. It was the
first time he had been on his own in the jungle so late.
Even the sun had gone to bed!

Suddenly it seemed very dark.

What was that?

Little Tiger looked up
and saw . . .

. . . two very large yellow eyes
staring back at him!

The eyes belonged to a bush baby.
"Shouldn't you be in bed?" she asked.
"I don't want to go to bed,"
said Little Tiger
bravely. "*You* haven't!"
"That's because I go to
bed when the sun rises,"
said Bush Baby.

"Fancy going to bed in the lovely sunshine!" thought Little Tiger. He shivered and thought how cold and dark it was in the jungle at night.

"I'm going to take you home," said Bush Baby.
"Your mummy and daddy will be worried about you."
    "I don't want to go home! I don't want to go to bed!"
said Little Tiger. But he didn't want to be left alone
in the dark either.

So Little Tiger followed Bush Baby through the jungle. He was glad of her big bright eyes to show him the way back home.

"We're nearly there," said Bush Baby, as Little Tiger's steps became slower and slower.

"I don't want to . . ." said Little Tiger sleepily,
dragging his paws.

"Ah, there you are," said Mummy Tiger.
"Just in time for bed!"

"I don't want to . . ." yawned Little Tiger,
and he fell fast asleep!
Mummy Tiger tucked him up
and then turned to Bush Baby . . .

. . . but the den was empty.
Bush Baby had disappeared into
the jungle before Mummy Tiger
could tuck *her* up, too!